HANSEL AND GRETEL

For *Ellen & Arthur Temple*

with love

First published 1997 by Walker Books Ltd
87 Vauxhall Walk, London SE11 5HJ

2 4 6 8 10 9 7 5 3 1

© 1997 Jane Ray

This book has been typeset in Benson Old Style.

Printed in Italy

British Library Cataloguing in Publication Data
A catalogue record for this book is
available from the British Library.

ISBN 0-7445-3787-8

HANSEL AND GRETEL

Retold and Illustrated by

JANE RAY

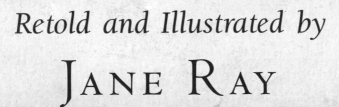

WALKER BOOKS
AND SUBSIDIARIES
LONDON • BOSTON • SYDNEY

On the edge of a great forest lived a poor woodcutter with his wife and his two children. The boy was called Hansel and the girl Gretel. The woodcutter had little enough to feed them all with and when a famine came to the land he was in despair.

"How can we feed the poor children when we have nothing even for ourselves?"

"There is only one thing to do," said his wife. "Early tomorrow morning we will take the children deep into the forest. We'll light a fire for them and we'll go off to our work and leave them. They will never find their way back home."

The woodcutter was horrified. "No," he said, "I cannot bear to leave my children."

"Then we must all starve," said the woman, and she gave him no peace until he agreed to her dreadful plan. Hansel and Gretel, who were unable to sleep for hunger, heard all that was said between their father and stepmother and clung together crying.

But Hansel had an idea, and when everyone was asleep he crept from the house and gathered up the little white pebbles that glowed like silver coins in the moonlight. He crammed as many as he could into his pockets, and went back to bed, whispering to Gretel that all would be well.

At break of day, before the sun had even risen, the woman came and shook the two children awake. She gave them each a tiny piece of bread and said, "Come now, we're off to the forest to chop wood."

They set off together down the path. As they walked, Hansel kept stopping and looking back. "Hansel," said his father. "What are you stopping for?"

"I am looking at my little white cat. It is sitting up on the roof saying goodbye to me." But Hansel was not looking at his cat — he was dropping the white pebbles one by one along the path.

When they reached the middle of the forest, the wood-cutter helped the children to build a fire of brushwood and pine cones, and when it was burning fiercely his wife said, "Sit down beside the fire, children, and rest. We are going to chop wood. When we've done we'll come back and fetch you."

Hansel and Gretel sat together by the fire and when midday came they ate their bread. After a while they fell asleep.

When they awoke it was dark and Gretel began to cry. Hansel comforted her. "Just wait until the moon rises and we'll soon find our way," he said. When the moon was up Hansel took his little sister by the hand and, sure enough, they found the pebbles, shining like brand new silver shillings, which showed them the way.

They walked all night long and at daybreak reached their home. Their stepmother was furious, but their father was overjoyed, for it had cut him to the heart to leave them behind alone.

Not long afterwards, another famine fell upon the land and again the children overheard their stepmother whispering her plan at night. "Everything is eaten; we have half a loaf left, and that is the end. The children must go. We will take them further into the wood, so that this time they will not find their way out."

Once again, Hansel crept from his bed to collect pebbles. But this time the door was locked and he could not get out. Still, he comforted his little sister and said, "Don't cry, Gretel. I'll think of something.

Go to sleep now."

Early the next morning, the woman woke them as before and gave them each a small piece of bread. On their way into the forest, Hansel crumbled the bread in his pocket and sprinkled bits along the path, looking back from time to time to check that the crumbs could be seen.

"Hansel, why do you stop and look round?" said his father.

"I am looking at my little pigeon. He's sitting on the roof saying goodbye to me," said Hansel.

"Fool!" said the woman. "That is not your little pigeon. It is the sun shining on the roof."

The woman led the children still deeper into the forest, where they had never in their lives been before.

The woodcutter again made a great fire and his wife said, "Just sit there, you children, and when you are tired you may sleep a little. We are going to cut wood, and in the evening when we are done, we will come back and fetch you."

At noon Gretel shared her bread with Hansel, who had scattered his along the way. Then they fell asleep. Evening passed, and no one came for the poor children. When they awoke it was dark. Hansel comforted his sister. "Just wait until the moon comes up, Gretel, then we'll see the little pieces of bread I scattered and they'll show us the way back home."

But when the moon rose there were no crumbs to be seen, for they had all been eaten by the forest birds. Hansel was afraid but he said bravely to Gretel, "Never mind, we will find the way."

The children walked all night long, and then all day, but by the next evening they were still deep in the forest and far, far from home. They were hungry, for they had nothing to eat but wild berries. They were so tired that their legs would barely carry them. At last they lay down under a tree in each other's arms and slept.

On the third day they started to walk again. They saw a beautiful snow-white bird singing so sweetly that they stopped to listen. It flapped its wings and flew off, leading them to a clearing in which there stood the most wonderful house they had ever seen.

The house was made of gingerbread, iced with pink and white sugar and covered all over with sweets and sugar plums. The window panes were of clear sugar and a fence made of little gingerbread figures ran around the house. The children gasped in amazement and then, because they were so hungry, began to break off handfuls of sugar, marzipan, chocolate and gingerbread.

Suddenly they heard a thin little voice from behind the window: "Nibble nibble, little mouse, who's that nibbling at my house?"

The children answered, "Just the winds, the winds that blow, from the sky to the earth below," and carried on eating. Gretel broke off a piece of gingerbread shutter and Hansel took a great bite from a roof tile made of candy.

Then the door opened and out came a woman as old as the hills, dressed in tatters with cobwebs and spiders clinging to her skirts.

Hansel and Gretel were so frightened they dropped the sweets they were nibbling. But the old woman held out her hands to them and said, "Dear little things, why don't you come inside and rest, for no one is going to harm you." She led them inside the gingerbread house and fed them on milk and pancakes, with sugar, apples and nuts. Then she showed them to two little beds made up with fresh white sheets. Hansel and Gretel climbed in and drifted to sleep, thinking they must be in heaven.

But the old woman who seemed so kind was really a witch. She had built the gingerbread house specially to lure the children to her. Witches have red eyes and can't see very far, but their sense of smell is as keen as an animal's, and they know when human beings are near. The witch liked children best of all. Whenever she caught one, she cooked it and ate it and considered it a grand feast.

In the morning, the witch crept into the sleeping children's room. She seized Hansel with her dry scaly hands, carried him off and locked him in a cage. He shouted and cried but it did no good. Then she went to Gretel, shook her awake and shouted at her, "Get up, lazybones, and make breakfast for your brother — I'm going to fatten him up. And when I've fattened him up I'll cook him and eat him."

Poor Gretel wept bitterly but she had to do as the witch said. Every day she made lots of fine things for Hansel to eat, while she herself got nothing but bones and scraps. And every day the old witch would go to the cage and call to Hansel, "Poke out your finger so that I may feel if you are fat enough yet." But Hansel had noticed that the witch could not see very well, and he poked out a little bone which fooled her.

After a few weeks, when Hansel didn't seem to be getting any fatter, the witch lost patience. "I will cook him tomorrow, fat or thin!" she said.

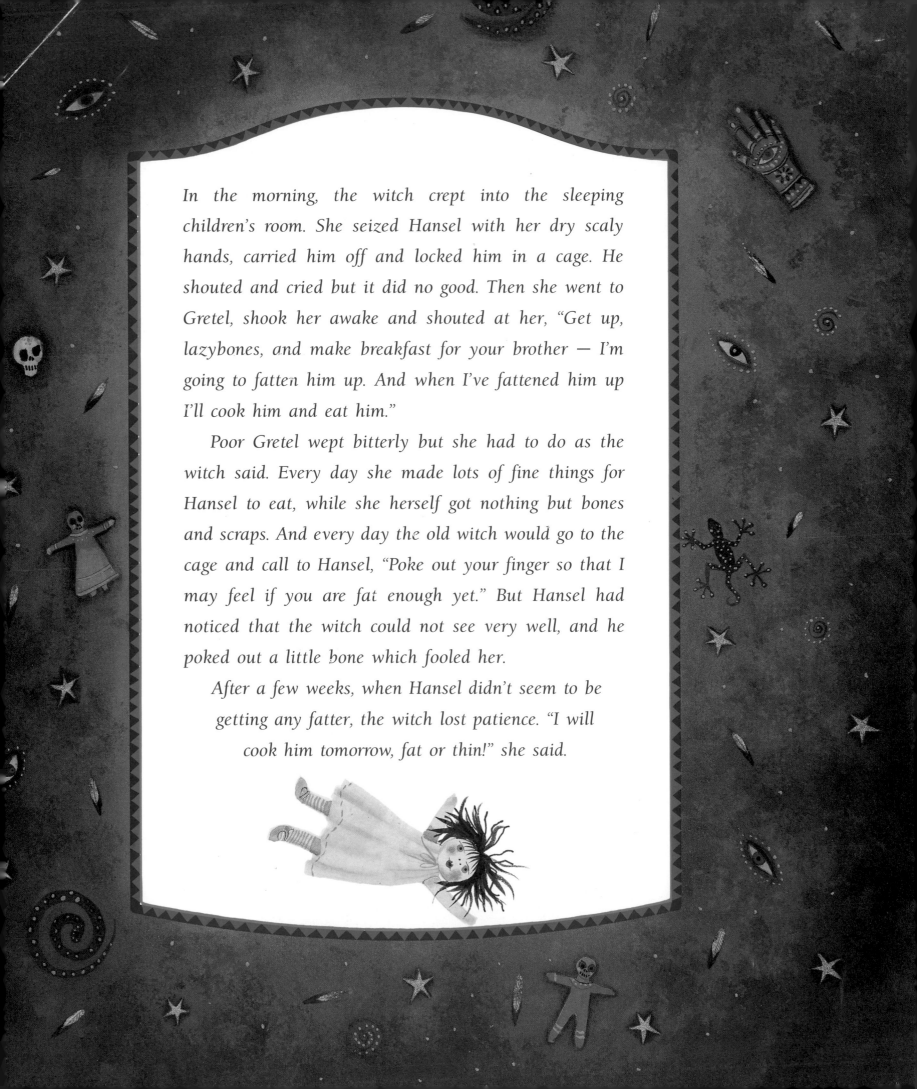

Early the next morning the witch called Gretel. "First we will bake," she said. "I have already kneaded the dough. Creep into the oven, Gretel, and see if it is hot enough." Once Gretel was inside, the old witch intended to slam the door and bake her too.

But Gretel was clever and saw what the witch had in mind. "I don't know what to do," she said. "How do I get in the oven?"

"You silly little goose," shouted the old woman. "Look, the door is plenty big enough — just climb in like this." The witch stuck in her head and Gretel, quick as lightning, pushed her as hard as she could into the oven and slammed and bolted the door.

That was the end of the witch.

Gretel ran to Hansel's cage and freed him. They hugged each other and danced and whooped with delight.

In every corner of the witch's house were chests full of gold and jewels. "These are far better than pebbles," said Hansel, and they stuffed their pockets full.

"Now we must be off," said Gretel. "We must find our way out of this forest."

When they had walked for hours they came to a great stretch of water. "How shall we cross?" said Hansel. "There is no bridge and no boat." But Gretel saw a little duck swimming by and called gently to her:

"Little duck, little duck, duckling dear,
Hansel and Gretel are standing here.
A bridge they lack and a boat they lack,
Please carry them over on your back."

The little duck swam up and took them over the water. They landed safely on the other side and walked on until the forest began to look more familiar.

At last they saw, far off, the woodcutter's house. Then they began to run and didn't stop running until they were in their father's arms. He was overjoyed to have his children back. Their stepmother had gone and now the three of them could live together in harmony, with gold and jewels enough to ensure that they never went hungry again.